HANNAH'S REDEMPTION

A Victorian Tale

TILLIE WALKER

Live Life Fully Media

ISBN: 978-1-63536-023-3

There wasn't much that tasted better than the first breath of air in the morning after stepping outside. Hannah drew it down into her lungs and smiled. It had rained in the night, and the London sky was washed fresh and bright and clean as a new bed sheet.

"Hannah!" Pa yelled, and she jumped. "Shut that blasted door, for goodness sake! And get to work."

She stepped over the threshold, slammed the door behind her, and started down the rickety steps that led from their rooms down into the courtyard.

Here the air took on a faint scent of urine that grew stronger as Hannah picked her way past the piles of broken fruit crates, squashed cabbage leaves, and loose straw scattered across the courtyard to reach the doorway and pass through to Weaver Street on the other side. Here the air was blended with the scents of coal smoke and horse manure, and as she walked briskly on towards Covent Garden, she took several long deep breaths, feeling the smoke and muck hang heavy in her lungs, trying to remind herself to be charitable, that it wasn't Pa's fault he was so out of sorts all the time, that he didn't mean to yell, that the morning breeze was very sharp and he had a right to not want it inside the room when he was trying to sleep.

But he didn't have to be such a tyrant about it. If she spoke to him like that, he wouldn't stand for it, it'd be the back of his hand and a violent curse flung at her, leaving her shaking and furious.

Ma wouldn't have let him act so. Ma had always made excuses for him, insisted it wasn't his fault and a man had a right to his temper, but she hadn't stood for it when he tried to take that temper out on Hannah. But Ma was dead three years now, and Pa's temper was only getting blacker.

She passed a rat catcher sitting in a doorway, his cages and poles in a clutter by his side. His black leather coat was spread out in front of him, and on it lay a small grey dog with woolly curls and floppy ears, nursing one fat white puppy. Hannah stopped and gazed at the scene for a moment, unable to stop the smile that spread over her face.

The rat catcher peered up at her from under the brim of his broken black topper. "Morning," he said.

"Morning," Hannah replied, and crouched down on her heels to gaze at the puppy. "Oh, it's so tiny."

"Yep. It's good they small, makes 'em fast and strong."

Hannah itched to run her fingers through the puppy's soft white coat, but she knew better than to disturb a nursing mother.

She gazed for a moment longer, then stood, grinned at the rat catcher, and carried on her way, feeling a little better about things. She squared her shoulders and lifted her chin. She just wouldn't think about it anymore. Pa just needed to find another job to work. It would probably be housebreaking, or roughing up some old cove in a dark alleyway, but it would be work, and it would mean he'd stop taking his anger out on everyone around him. He might even smile and give

Hannah a shilling that she could squirrel away into her tiny savings fund. Not that he knew about the fund. He probably thought she'd spend her money on drink, or maybe a new ribbon for her bonnet.

She touched her hair quickly to reassure herself, adjusting one of the pins keeping her brown chip bonnet in place. She'd sewn a red ribbon around the crown last year, and now it was worn thin and smooth, hence the need for hair pins to keep it on her head. If she could make do with pins, then that was a sixpence she could keep safe and quiet in the battered black purse she'd hidden behind a loose brick in the wall by her old straw tick mattress.

A boy ran past her, bumping against the flower basket she carried over her arm.

"Oi!" she yelled after him, but he just stuck up two fingers at her and carried on.

She wouldn't think about Pa anymore, or money, or the future. She had work to do.

❧

"SWEET VIOLETS!" HANNAH'S VOICE WAS GROWING HOARSE already, and it wasn't even past noon. "Sweet violets, penny a bunch!"

She'd moved away from Covent Garden, preferring to walk the streets in a more residential area. Not so posh that she'd be asked to leave, but well-to-do enough that the bankers and grocers who lived there could afford to spend their money on posies and ribbons.

She was walking with Margaret, another flower girl much younger than herself. Margaret's voice was fresher than Hannah's, and she had a rosy twinkle about her that customers found endearing. They'd teamed up a few years ago when Hannah had started to notice a change in the people asking her for flowers. When she was younger, it had been all right. Elderly gentlemen buying little nosegays for their buttonholes, middle-aged women calling her "poor dear lamb" as they handed over their pennies, sometimes children not much older than herself but markedly better off asking their parents loudly, "Mama, can I buy a flower from the poor little girl?"

But now that she was seventeen she noticed that the rich huddled their children close by them when she came near, and said things like, "Don't look at her, Clarence. Come along, Mary, don't stare."

The elderly gentlemen, gravely kind and sometimes even courteous when she was younger, now wouldn't even look at the flowers she tried to offer them. But sometimes they looked at *her*, at her body inside her rough black dress, and even as their lips curled in disgust their eyes begged her to come nearer. She knew what they thought. A woman might call herself a flower girl, but too often that was just a cover up for her real profession, the oldest one in the book. It was fine when a girl was little, but it was different when they got older.

She'd tried to say this to Pa, but he wouldn't listen. "If you don't act like you're cheap, they won't think you're cheap. Have you been acting like you're cheap?"

"No Pa, but – "

"No buts. If you ain't acting like it, they won't think it. And we need the money."

Hannah shook her head. That was why walking with Margaret was good. Margaret was ten, still young enough to walk without suspicion, and when Hannah walked with her, people's gazes were a little kinder, a little less quick to judge.

Margaret was chattering on about the latest addition to her family, twin boys who had just been named Peter and Herbert.

"... and Herbert, he's the one with the hair, he was sick all down his front, and lordy, it smelled just like cheese, like someone'd taken a block of it and crumbled it all down his front. But then they always smell like cheese anyway. Peter, he's never sick, but he still smells like cheese. If you sniff the back of his head where it's all soft, it smells so strong." She giggled. "He's going bald, Peter is. On the back of his head, like an old man."

"Bald?"

"Yeah. Ma said it's normal, though, she said it's because of how his head rubs against her arm when she holds him." Margaret mimed holding a baby in her arms, shifting her flower basket back into the dip of her elbow. "See?"

"Yes, I see. I didn't have any brothers or sisters, so I s'pose otherwise I'd have seen it too." Hannah grinned down at Margaret. "Little bald babies. Babies are funny."

Margaret considered this seriously for a moment. "I don't know. I think I should like to have one, one day. Just one, though, not tons and tons like Ma has. Ma's always having babies, so she never gets to do anything else. She just gets fat and cross and heavy and swears a lot. And then she's in bed for ages, and then the baby comes, and then Ma gets fat again."

The innocent look on Margaret's face sent a little chill down Hannah's back. Of course Margaret was too young to know about families, and what exactly happened between a man and a woman. It wasn't Hannah's place to tell her. That would be up to her mother. But would she tell her? Ma hadn't told Hannah anything. It was only when Hannah's bleeding started and Ma noticed that she'd reluctantly given her a few details. But, considering what Hannah had learned later when she'd asked among the other flower girls, Ma hadn't told her anything useful at all. Maybe it wasn't proper or decent to talk about it. But Hannah was glad she knew. It would keep her safe, keep her careful.

She glanced down at Margaret's face, so young and round, whipped pink by the wind and the sun. Her hair, springing free from either side of her soft cap, was blonde and curly, and shone in the sunlight. It wouldn't be long now before the elderly gentlemen started looking at her in the same way they looked at Hannah.

"Listen, Margaret – " she began.

"Oo! Look!" Margaret pointed excitedly at a horse and rider trotting down the road towards them.

The horse was striking, shining chestnut brown under the sun, beautifully groomed and saddled with a red leather harness studded with silver points. Its rider was a woman, a lady, wearing all red – a long red skirt, a tight red jacket, and a tiny red hat with a long black feather pinned to the front of her head. She sat the horse proudly, fiercely, and she gazed straight ahead with her back as straight as a fence post.

"So pretty," Margaret murmured.

"She's not a lady," Hannah heard herself say. "Not a decent one. Decent folk don't wear red. And decent women don't strut about like that."

Margaret peered up at her, frowning. "What?"

Hannah was silent, her father's words burning in her mouth.

"Hannah?" Margaret prodded. Hannah swallowed hard. Margaret turned back with a sigh. "Well, *I* think she's pretty, *and* the horse, *and* her red hat."

Maybe the lady heard them, or maybe she simply wanted flowers, but she drew her horse to a halt in front of them and looked down. "Violets, are they?" Her voice was light and clipped, and as proud as the rest of her. "I'll take two bunches."

"Thank you, missus!" Margaret beamed up at her.

"Thank you, missus," Hannah said automatically, and held up the flowers.

The lady took them, and her soft black riding glove touched Hannah's fingers briefly. Then she tucked the flowers into the bosom of her jacket, gathered up the reins, and trotted away down the street.

Margaret gazed after her adoringly. "So pretty."

"You've said that a thousand times already," Hannah snapped, and immediately regretted it when she saw Margaret's hurt little face. "I'm sorry." She tried to laugh. "I'm sorry. I don't know what got into me. I just – I don't know. I'm sorry."

They walked on, but now there was a silence between them. Margaret looked down at her feet, and her voice no longer had the same chirp to it as before. Hannah tried desperately to think of something to say to distract her.

She saw a gentleman a little way ahead of them, pausing by a side corner to light a cigarette. She glanced back at Margaret, but she was still looking at her feet, and starting to lag behind.

Hannah put a smile on her face and marched up to the gentleman. "Sweet violets, sir? Penny a bunch?"

The gentleman discarded the spent lucifer and exhaled deeply, examining her through the cloud of blue smoke.

"A penny?" His voice was rich and low.

Hannah tried not to choke on the smoke and keep her smile in place. "Just a penny, sir. They look so pretty on a lapel, or they make a lovely gift for a sweetheart. Would you like to smell one?"

He laughed. "Would I like to smell one?" He rested his hand on the edge of Hannah's basket, the weight of it threatening to spill the contents over the road. "I'll tell you what I'd like." He lunged forward, his hand leaping from the basket to Hannah's arm, dragging her towards him. "I'd like to smell *you*, little flower girl, that's what I'd like."

❧ 2 ❧

Hannah's mind went completely blank. She felt the man's hand twisting her arm, she felt his hot breath and the stink of cigarette smoke on her face, and for one second she looked into his eyes and noticed, quite calmly, that they were blue.

Then her mind whirred back into life. She tried to break free, but the man's grip was too strong. Her basket dropped to the ground, flowers scattering all around them.

The man laughed, saying, "Oh come now, *flower girl*, I know your kind." He wrenched her arm down so that her shoulder cried out in pain, and his other hand was on her neck, on her throat, crushing her so she couldn't breathe.

Hannah brought her knee up between the man's legs. Her skirts hampered the move, but it was enough to make his grip loosen. He made a strange gasping sound, and she slapped him, hard across the jaw, and then again across his ear, and he staggered back from her.

Hannah realised Margaret was there, pulling at her arm, crying, "Come on, come on, Hannah, we have to go!"

Hannah let herself be pulled back. She grabbed up her

basket, and then she and Margaret were running down the street, back towards Covent Garden. She heard the man shouting after them, yelling curses and threats, but they didn't stop running.

As they got closer to home, they slowed their pace. They were near the corner where Margaret and Hannah usually went their separate way.

"Wait," Hannah said, as she stopped to catch her breath and listen for footsteps behind them. Once she was satisfied that the man was no longer following them, she said, "Go directly home, Margaret. Now."

Margaret nodded and started to run again, towards the row house where her family squeezed themselves into two rooms, without looking back. Hannah watched her until she was sure she was out of danger, then certain she heard footsteps getting closer, started to run again.

❦

HANNAH'S BOOTS THUDDED ON THE WOODEN STAIRCASE, and she burst into the room so violently the door flew back and crashed into the back wall.

"Hannah!" Pa roared from the bed. "What did I tell you about coming in like a tempest, girl!"

Hannah ignored him. It took her three tries to unknot her bonnet ribbon, and she jammed it on the hook and began to fumble with her shawl. Her hands were still shaking. Her heart was beating out a hot scared rhythm in her ears. She realised that Pa was yelling at her still, but it seemed to be happening very far away and she couldn't concentrate on his voice at all.

She sat down on the little stool in the corner and stared at the rough grey floorboards past her knees. She should take her boots off. She should start dinner. It was early yet, but at least she'd get a head start on the soup. There was a bit of cabbage left over from yesterday, and she could throw in that old bit of mutton and potato, if Pa hadn't eaten them already.

Pa's hand landed on her shoulder. She started, and gave a little cry.

"Hannah," Pa crouched down in front of her, peering at her from underneath his heavy dark brows. His eyes were bleary but concerned as he scratched his thick black beard. "Hannah, my girl. What's amiss?"

The sight of him bent down, stooped to be on her level, as though she were a little girl again and he was about to comfort her in the old easy way, was too much for Hannah. She hadn't cried a drop on the way back, had dried Margaret's tears and comforted her easily enough, but now she covered her face with her hands and burst into desperate sobs.

Pa pulled her into a hug that crushed her nose against his shoulder. His big hand cupped the back of her head, ruffling her hair. "There, there," he murmured, just like he used to do when she was little. He held her as she cried and cried, and then, when she was a mess of tears and snot, he released her, and she sat back limply on the stool and wiped her eyes on the back of her wrist.

"Here." Pa passed her a handkerchief.

She took it, noting dully that it was silk and had a strange monogram embroidered in one corner. But she blew her nose and wiped her eyes, and felt a little better.

"There, now," Pa said. "What's amiss, Hannah?"

"I..." She twisted the handkerchief in her lap. "I can't be a flower girl anymore, Pa. I just can't. It's not like it was. It's not sweet anymore. People look at me and they think ...." Her voice trailed off and she gulped before she continuing. "I know you said if I don't act like it they won't think it, but that's not true, they do think it and it's not because of anything I do, it's just how they think."

Pa shook his head. "We've had this talk before, Hannah, and you know what I said."

"But I can't!" Her voice rose. "I can't do it anymore!"

"Hush!" Pa's voice met hers, and he stood up. "Don't you take that tone with me. I'm your pa, and I say what goes here."

"No!" Hannah took a breath, terrified at the expression on Pa's face. But she had to carry on. "No, you don't understand, Pa. I can't do it anymore. I won't. I – " She swallowed. "I know you're my pa. I know all that. But I can't do it anymore. It's not – safe anymore."

Pa stared down at her, and a strange grimace twisted his mouth.

"I'll get a job. I'm old enough now. I saw a sign in the baker's shop for an apprentice. I'd like that."

"The baker isn't going to hire the likes of you, girl. They want respectable folk."

The suggestion from her own Pa that she wasn't respectable stung as if he had slapped her.

"I'll do anything else, Pa" Hannah rushed on. "Anything else that isn't – that doesn't – something appropriate. I'll work hard and I'll mind you and I'll – but I can't be a flower girl anymore."

Pa nodded slowly.

Hannah blew her nose again, trying to catch her breath. Sounds of the streets beyond the courtyard filtered through the half-open window with the grey sunlight: the clop and scrape of horse hooves, the rattle of cartwheels, the yell of the coster boys. Hannah closed her eyes, and her breath fluttered in her throat.

"All right." Pa stepped back and sat on the bed. "You don't have to be a flower girl anymore."

Hannah's heart trembled, and she felt the tears close again.

"You're going to help me instead." He was nodding, thinking to himself. "There's a house in Marylebone I've had my eye on. Jack and Pat and me was going to turn it over, but now... Won't have to split it three ways. Keep it all ourselves."

"Pa – "

"Some fat grocer with more money than he's a right to. Just a tradesman what got lucky. There's a pantry window, too small for me, but you should be able to squeeze in."

"Pa." Hannah swallowed. "Pa, please."

He scowled. "You said, Hannah. You said you'd do anything."

"I know, but – please, Pa. You know I don't like – I don't think it's right – "

"*You* don't think it's *right*?" Suddenly he was off the bed and standing over her. "Oh, so because poor little miss doesn't think it's *right* and *good* and *proper* we should all starve in our beds, is that it?"

"No, that's not ... "

He grabbed her arm and hauled her to her feet. Her shoulder gave a painful twinge and she gasped, but he ignored her. "Don't you bloody dare look down your nose at me, my girl. We all have our trades, and seeing as how you're too high and mighty to keep down the one you had, you're going to have to make do, and you're going to do it without whining and crying, you understand me? I'm your pa, and you're going to do what I say, when I say, how I say, and if you don't like it you can bloody well keep your trap shut and count your blessings I don't send you out to walk the streets like some fathers might with a lazy good-for-nothing daughter who refuses to work. *Do you understand me?*"

Hannah couldn't hold his furious black gaze. She nodded, staring past his elbow to look at the floor.

"Good." He released her, and stamped back to the bed. "We'll head out as soon as it's dark. Get the dinner on now so we can eat before we go." He stretched out on the bed and pulled the blankets over his head.

Slowly, Hannah moved to the cupboard. She took out the cabbage, the tiny pot with the scraps of meat and potato, the old copper kettle, and the spoon. She felt strange and detached from the rest of herself. She looked down at her hands, and they seemed to belong to someone very different, someone unfamiliar and very tired. But the scalding tracks of tears down her cheeks were real, and hot, and she couldn't make them stop.

Hannah lingered over the soup for as long as she dared. The Evans family downstairs in the bigger room had a fireplace, and they always let her use it to cook when they weren't using it. The Evanses were jolly and cheerful, a young couple come from Wales to work in the city, with a growing crop of jolly cheerful children who spoke cockney-accented English with soft pretty Welsh phrases dropped in here and there. The newest addition to their family looked up at Hannah, gurgled and smiled, so Hannah lifted her up.

Hannah held the baby in her arms, rocking it gently while she watched the soup simmer and Mrs Evans worked with the other three children on building lucifer boxes. Mrs Evans had clearly noticed the tear marks on Hannah's face earlier, and looked at her questioningly, but Hannah only ducked her head and mumbled something about soup.

That had been an hour ago, and still Hannah hadn't found the courage to go back upstairs. She imagined herself part of this loving family as she moved from side to side in steady rhythm, as if she was standing on the deck of a ship, the baby content and sleeping in her arms. She heard a footstep behind her.

"That soup must be boiled to kingdom come," Mrs Evans said. She touched Hannah's shoulder lightly, and Hannah flinched.

"I know. I'm sorry. I'll be going back soon."

"Hannah, dear, what's wrong? It's not like you to spoil a soup. You're a good cook."

Hannah shook her head. She looked up into Mrs Evans' kind worried face, and tried to smile. "Nothing. It's fine. I'm fine. I've had a rough day, is all."

Mrs Evans raised an eyebrow. "You know you can always talk to me, pet. I'm always here. Daffyd, stop poking your sister and get back to work."

"I know. Thank you." Hannah stared into the fireplace, at the little low flames crackling blue and orange around the log. The light on the sides of the fat kettle was warm and orange, the shadows very black and deep. She could do this. She could. It was just for tonight, and then she'd go out and try to find some other work, and then Pa couldn't force her to do anymore for him. It would be fine. It was just this one night.

She closed her eyes. She thought of the gentleman from earlier, with his blue cigarette smoke and his mocking laughter. Housebreaking was better than that. Anything was better than that.

It took more courage than she thought she possessed, but she made herself stand up. The baby stirred in her arms, blinking, and it yawned, showing its pink little tongue like a kitten. She held it close for a second, breathing in the sweet smell of its head, and she thought of Margaret, and she made herself remember the gentleman, the hungry look in his eyes and the careless easy power in his hands.

"I'm going now," she said, as she carefully laid the baby in Mrs Evans' arms, and unhooked the kettle from the spit.

Mrs Evans saw her to the door. "Take care of yourself," she said, and propping the baby up on her shoulder, she pulled her into a careful one-armed hug.

"I will," Hannah said.

Back upstairs, Pa was awake and pulling on his boots. "There are you," he grunted. "Thought you'd gone and run away."

Hannah said nothing, but set the kettle down and found two bowls. She poured out the soup and handed Pa one bowl, and took the other for herself. They ate in silence, Pa only commenting once that the soup tasted like it had been boiled to within an inch of its life and if she couldn't do better with what he provided there was no point in saving the mutton and he'd just as rather have it in his lunch sandwich.

Hannah said nothing.

After dinner, Pa said he was going out to get a few things. Hannah nodded and sat on the stool, gazing out of the window at the fading light. The sky was grey and purple above the chimney tops, black coal smoke hung heavy in the air and turned the light of the sunset fiercely red and orange. Maybe she should run away. She had no idea where she'd go. Maybe the Evanses would take her in. No, that wasn't fair to ask. Offering a sympathetic ear wasn't the same as offering a place to live, and even if it were she'd still need to find a trade. Besides, moving downstairs wasn't far enough away. Pa would just storm down and drag her back.

Maybe she could find work in a shop somewhere. But shop girls were a different class, they were snooty and spoke posh and had posh clothes. If she used all her savings she could probably get a new dress, something real nice and proper, but then what? A new dress didn't mean she'd be guaranteed a job, and if she didn't get one she'd be worse off than when she started, starving to death but looking fine while doing so.

Hannah grinned weakly to herself, and sighed. It was too hard and too depressing to think about what might or not be. This was when she could see where Pa was coming from. You can put a pig in a dress and call it Clarence, Pa used to say, but it's still just a pig in a dress. People were born where they were meant to be, and no good came of trying to jump up to places where you didn't belong.

Hannah thought back to Pa's derisive words about the grocer – *"more money than he's a right to"* – and a sick feeling began to creep into her stomach. She couldn't do this. It was wrong. It was beyond wrong, it went against everything Hannah believed and had fought against for years. Ever since Ma died, Pa had been dropping hints how Hannah should start helping him out on jobs. Hannah had flatly refused, and received more than one box around the ears for doing so. This was way back before the Evanses had moved in, and the family who'd lived there before had a daughter who was older than Hannah who worked as a flower girl. She'd taken Hannah under her wing, and with both girls' enthusiasm and the fact that Hannah proved a very good saleswoman, Pa had reluctantly agreed to the whole thing.

And she was a good saleswoman. The fact that even now, with the shadow of an older flower girl's reputation looming over, she still managed to earn enough for their meals and put a few pence by for her savings proved that.

The orange light was bleeding down the sky behind the black shapes of the rooftops, and Hannah could see the faint glow of the moon beginning, though smudged and blurred by the smoke in the air. Her hands were cold. She'd need her shawl tonight.

The absurdity of that thought made her suddenly laugh aloud, even as tears sprang to her eyes. Why was she thinking about her shawl, as though she were about to go on an evening walk? This was ridiculous. This was mad. This was wrong. She couldn't do it.

Hannah sprang to her feet, almost over-turning the tiny stool, but as she reached for the handle, the door swung open and Pa stood in the threshold. He glowered at her. "Where you going?"

"Nowhere." Her voice sounded weak and thin, like a fragile cotton thread, and she hated herself for it.

"Good. You'd better not be getting any ideas in your head, my girl." Pa slid the rough black bag off his shoulder. It hit the floor with a heavy metallic thud, and he rubbed the back of his neck. "Well, get a move on then. You ready?"

Hannah picked up her shawl from her bed, and wrapped it about her shoulders and waist. She felt as though she were watching all this happen to someone else, someone else called Hannah who was wearing the same thick grey shawl with the red trim but who knew what she was doing and didn't have a horrible queasy fear rising up inside her.

Pa heaved the bag onto his back, grunting as he settled it against his spine. He put a heavy hand on Hannah's shoulder, and pushed her towards the door. "Come on. Pick up your feet."

Outside the air was cool and smoky. Hannah breathed in without thinking, but even the rush of cold air in her lungs seemed to be happening to someone else. Pa led the way down the steps and out into the street.

There was a gang of boys scuffling on the corner, and a few stopped to watch them go by, staring at them with hungry, guarded faces.

They have no idea what we're going to do, Hannah thought. Or maybe they do. Maybe they can see it on our faces. Maybe I already look like a criminal. A housebreaker. A thief.

"Don't drag behind," Pa growled.

They passed a few night stalls, fishmongers selling their wares by candlelight. The light gleamed bronze on the silver scales of herrings and mackerel and sardines, and the pungent smell mingled with that rising from the coffee cart parked a little further down. A man with a tray of ham sandwiches approached them, but Pa snapped "No!" so savagely that the man almost tripped over his own feet stepping back in surprise. Hannah shot him an apologetic smile as they hurried on.

They walked on and on, Hannah sometimes running to keep up with Pa's longer stride. The sky above was now black, and heavy with clouds, and as they moved away from the shops and stalls, the only light came from the lampposts, glowing with a warm yellow light.

Pa abruptly turned down a small side street, and they came out by a row of terraced houses. There were no lampposts here, and the only light came from one house in the middle where the curtains had not yet been drawn in the downstairs window. Pa flung out an arm, stopping Hannah in her tracks. "Wait," he hissed, and pulled her back into the shadows.

Hannah leaned against the wall. Pa's back was a strange lumpy shape in the dark, distorted by the bag, but she could see the tension in his shoulders as he stared up at the solitary lit window.

For a long time they stood there silently, Pa staring unmoving at the window, Hannah gazing up at the sky. She closed her eyes against the breeze, and shivered slightly. The sick feeling in her stomach was fading away, leaving in its place a kind of cool numb distance. She should be nervous. She should be worrying about the pantry window, about falling over, about making a noise. But her head felt empty, as if every thought and worry had been wiped away with a damp cloth.

Pa's hand gripped her wrist. The window was dark. He pulled her away from the wall, and ducking low, they ran across the road to the house at the far end of the terrace.

❧ 4 ☙

"**D**own here." Pa pushed Hannah around the corner to where a short wooden fence joined onto the row of houses. He bent down and cupped his hands to make a step, and hoisted her over the fence. She heard her skirt catch on something and rip, but she landed quietly, knees bent. Pa followed, but the bag caught against the fence post and made the tools inside ring out with a great jangling clang that sounded like a house falling down.

They both crouched low for a second, frozen against the cold earth. Hannah's heart was hammering in her ears, but she felt strangely calm as she strained her ears for any sound that meant they'd been discovered.

After a long pause, Pa's hand found Hannah's arm in the dark. He gave it a shake, and they began to creep forward again. Hannah caught up the torn edge of her skirt and held it in her hand, her fingers working the ragged threads. She'd have to mend it when she got home. Did she have enough black thread? She thought so, but she'd had to mend Pa's jacket the other week, and that had been a big job. Maybe she'd have to get some more. Would Pa give her the money? Probably not.

Get a grip, she told herself sternly. *Concentrate. You're robbing a house, for goodness sake. Stop thinking about thread.*

This row of houses each had a tiny yard behind it, more of a space for the kitchen maid to throw out the dirty water than anything else, though the yard they were in did have a few pots of what looked like herbs, and some other shrubby bushes Hannah couldn't make out properly in the dark.

Pa was right up against the back wall of the house. He found her arm again and dragged her to him. He opened the bag and took out a covered lantern. He fumbled for a moment with the matches, then lit the lamp and shone the light up the wall. He pointed, and Hannah was able to make out a shape that might be a window.

He pulled her head close, his voice a hot hoarse whisper in her ear. "That's the pantry window. I came by the other day and fixed the latch, so it'll push open no trouble. I'll boost you up."

Hannah found herself staring at the heavy mass of his beard and wondering if he'd grown it on purpose so he would be difficult to identify if he ever had to go on the run. Though he could always just use a false beard. Maybe Ma had liked it.

Pa's fingers dug into her arm. "Don't you dare make a mess of this, my girl. Get yourself up there and do what I told you."

Hannah nodded. Pa hoisted her up, and she scrambled for a grip, almost kicking him in the face. He grabbed her ankle and placed it on his shoulder, and she reached for the edge of the windowsill. The window was tiny, but Hannah was small, and straight and flat as a stick. She pulled it open, and began to squeeze carefully in. The room was dark, even darker it seemed than the night outside, and Hannah paused a moment, still half-in and half-out of the window, allowing her eyes to adjust to the gloom. The air smelled heavy and savoury and a bit smoky. There was a shelf directly below the window which she grabbed to steady herself, and she saw a little further along the shapes of things that looked like a ham, a round wheel of cheese, and a meaty joint of beef with the bone sticking up like a strange little scarecrow.

Something – Pa's impatient hand – grabbed her ankle and shoved her forward. She stifled a cry, catching at the shelf below to stop herself toppling onto the floor. One of her flailing arms struck the ham and sent it flying over the edge. It hit the flagstones below with a dull thud.

Hannah's heart was hammering, and her breath came in gasps. She twisted along the shelf, into the empty space where the ham had been, and pulled herself further through the window, banging her knee on the sill and almost falling over the edge again until she was all the way through, crouched on the top shelf among the dried meat and cheese. The shelves creaked under her weight, and she slid carefully down to the floor.

Hannah's eyes had adjusted to the dark, and she could see the pantry door just a few steps away. She reached for the handle, and crept out into a wide, shadowy kitchen. She stepped carefully on the floor, making sure her boots didn't ring out on the flagstones. There was a large wooden commode on the other side of the room, lined with white plates that gave off a faint milky glow in the gloom, and next to the dresser was a door that must open out to the back yard.

A low growl reverberated through the kitchen. Out of the shadows by the range stepped a dog. It was small, pale, and wiry, and its teeth were bared, its short bristling tail held high. It took a slow, stiff-legged step towards her.

Slowly, carefully, Hannah knelt down on the floor. She

placed her hands on her knees, palms upward, and gazed at a spot on the floor to the left. "It's all right," she breathed. "It's all right. Please don't bark."

The dog growled again, and took another step forward.

"Please don't bark. If you bark then the whole house will hear and I'll get caught, and I really don't want to get caught. Or even if I don't get caught, Pa will be so cross, and I don't know what I'll do then. Please don't bark. I'm not going to hurt you." Hannah tried to keep her voice low and soft, and her posture unthreatening. "I know, I'm a strange person in the middle of the night. And I'm not here to do anything good or kind, I'm breaking in to steal things. But it's not like that's what I want to do. It's Pa, Pa's the one making me do it. Please don't bark."

She risked glancing up. The dog was still staring at her. She met its eyes and looked hastily away, then back again.

Slowly, cautiously, it wagged its tail.

"Good boy," Hannah breathed. "That's it. I'm a friend. Look, come see." Very slowly she extended her hand, and the dog came and sniffed her palm. It wagged its tail again, and sniffed her wrist, then up her arm. Hannah lightly touched its chest and stroked its coarse hair. "Good boy," she whispered, and its tail wagged again.

Very slowly, she stood up. The dog backed away, but when she bent over and offered her hand again, it came and sniffed her, and seemed satisfied.

Hannah glanced behind her. "Come on," she whispered, and opened the pantry door. She picked up the ham from the floor, and held it in front of the dog's nose. The dog sniffed it eagerly, and tried to snatch it from her hand.

She held it up out of its reach, and in response, the dog sat up and begged, its head tipped to one side and its pink tongue lolling out of the opposite side of its mouth.

It looked so darling that Hannah's heart melted. "Oh,

you're so sweet," she breathed, and found herself almost laughing at the sight.

The dog gave a little whine of eagerness, and she came back to herself.

She tossed the ham into the far corner of the pantry underneath the shelves, and while the dog dived for it, she stepped hastily back into the kitchen, shut the door, fastening it shut before unlatching the kitchen door to the alley where Pa was waiting.

"Why were you so long?" Pa hissed when she opened the back door. "What happened, what's wrong?"

"Dog," she whispered back. "I shut it up in the pantry."

He grunted, and held the lantern up. Its dim light caught on the copper kettles and pans hanging from the ceiling, and sent fantastic spiked shadows up the wall from the herbs on the drying rack suspended above the huge kitchen table. He moved carefully to where there were two doors set in the wall, and set to work examining the lock on the smaller one, then, taking something from the bag, carefully picked it open. The lantern light gleamed on a case full of silverware set against the back wall of the tiny room, which looked like an office of some kind.

Pa bent to work with his lock pick on the cabinet and hissed, "Have a look round, see what you can find."

There was a small desk set against one wall, holding a carafe of something Hannah guessed was brandy, a heavy ledger, an ink pot, and a pen. She tried the drawers, but their only contents were more pens and some blotting paper.

Next to the case of silverware was a small bureau, and when Hannah tried these drawers, they slid open to reveal trays of silver cutlery. She glanced at Pa, wondering if she dared stay silent, but he had already looked around and seen her discovery.

"Bag it," he hissed, and so she began gathering up handfuls of shiny knives and forks and spoons, and dumping them into the sack.

She wondered whether the dog had finished the ham yet. Maybe she should make an excuse to go and check on it, sit with it and feed it to keep it quiet. That wouldn't be so bad, if she spent the entire robbery in the pantry sharing the meat and cheese with the dog.

"Pa," she began, but he waved his arm impatiently at her. She bit her lip, and glanced behind her at the kitchen. The other door must lead out into the rest of the house. She hoped Pa would be satisfied with the kitchen and not venture out further, but she had a sinking doubt that he would not be so sensible.

The door of the cabinet clicked open, and Pa gestured her closer, and began filling the bag with plates, a milk jug, a sugar pot, an entire tea service.

"It's too heavy," she whispered, but he just shook his head at her and scowled. "I can't carry it," she tried again, and he hissed back,

"'Course you can't, stupid girl, I'm carrying it."

"Pa, I think I should check on the dog."

"You're not going anywhere."

"But what if it starts barking again."

"You stay where you are."

Hannah fell silent, and watched numbly as Pa placed the last plate in the sack. He hissed, "We'll leave the bag by the door and have a quick look around the rest."

"Pa, no – "

"Shut up."

Hannah tried to think of something to say that would convince him. She looked up, and saw him freeze in his place, his eyes wide. She turned around to follow his gaze.

A small girl stood in the doorway, watching them with huge round eyes. She wore a long white nightgown, and her hair was tied up in a multitude of curl papers, making her small round head look spiked like a hedgehog.

She stared at them, and said in a small voice, "You're not allowed in there. That's Mr Collins' room."

"That's right," Hannah said quickly, "We aren't going in there. We're going to go now."

The little girl looked past Hannah, stared at Pa, and her lower lip began to tremble. As the realisation came to her that something was amiss, she sucked in her breath and formed her lips into a tiny 'O' as she prepared to scream.

Hannah turned back to Pa, and saw his expression harden. "Pa, no!" she whispered, but it was too late.

In a split second, Pa shoved Hannah out of the way, sending her sprawling, and grabbed the little girl around the waist. She let loose one startled cry, but Pa smothered it under his hand. He bundled her roughly up under one arm like a load of dirty washing, grabbed Hannah's arm, and dragged them both across the kitchen and bundled them into the pantry.

"Pa – " Hannah gasped.

The dog leapt up in fright and began barking, discarding the half-eaten ham. Pa let out a furious curse and dragged them back out into the kitchen, but the dog followed them, barking frantically.

"Shh," Hannah pleaded, trying to reach for it, but Pa hauled her back.

"Grab the bag," he ordered. "Game's up."

The dog lunged forward. Pa swung the little girl up out of the way, and kicked the dog in the ribs. Its bark broke off into a high squeal of pain. The little girl wriggled her face free and screamed, "Sammy!"

Pa swore again, and let loose a furious frustrated volley of kicks into the dog's side. It cried, whimpering horribly, and tried to crawl away, but Pa followed with another kick.

The little girl was screaming.

Hannah realised she was weeping without tears, her throat hoarse, crying, "No, no, no, no, no."

Upstairs, someone shouted. Swift footsteps thudded over the ceiling above them.

"Bag!" Pa was yelling at her. "Grab the bag!"

The bag was still lying by the door on the opposite side of the room.

Pa swung out furiously, and slapped Hannah's face so hard her ears rang, and for a moment she thought she might faint. "Come on!" He dragged her towards the kitchen door. The little girl was still under his arm; she was still screaming, crying out for her mother.

Pa and Hannah fled across the yard. Pa dropped the girl for a moment to hoist Hannah over the fence, and then grabbed the child again and almost threw her over into Hannah's arms. Hannah staggered back under her weight, but then Pa was there, and he took her again, flinging her over his shoulder. He grabbed Hannah's arm with his free hand, and they were running away from the house with its lighted windows and its outcry. Over all the tumult, Hannah thought she heard a woman screaming.

5

When they had run enough of a distance, and Pa had taken them down so many side alleys and twists and turns that Hannah had completely lost her bearings, they stopped for a moment to catch their breath.

The little girl had stopped screaming, but was still crying huge hiccupping sobs from being jounced up and down on Pa's shoulder.

Pa took her down roughly and set her on her feet. "All right, nipper. Now you do what you're told and you won't get hurt, you understand me?"

The child just stared at him. Her mouth was wide open, every breath half a gasping wheezing wail, and her face was covered with a glossy shining web of snot and tears.

Pa shook her, and her sobs change to gasping coughs.

"Stop it! You're going to make her choke," Hannah said. Her own face was wet. Her eyes felt crusty and sore.

Pa snorted. "Don't you act like I don't know how to handle little 'uns. Raised you, didn't I?"

He grabbed the child's wet chin and forced her face up to

meet his. "Look at me. Properly. That's it. Now." He dug his fingers into her cheeks. "You're going to be a good girl, you hear me? You're going to be good. You're going to be quiet. You're going to do what you're told. And nothing bad will happen to you. You understand that?"

The child blinked once, then gave a tiny nod.

"Good." Pa released her face, and stood up. "No more crying, understand? You're going to be a good girl."

"Pa." Hannah's throat was hoarse. "Pa, what are you going to do?"

The alleyway they stood in was dark, with only a faint yellow light shining in from the lamppost at the opposite end. Pa's face was a jaundiced blur of skin and shadows, but Hannah could hear the disdain in his voice.

"Well, seeing as how someone completely muffed up their part tonight and left the bag of goods behind, we've got to make do with what we got, don't we."

"Pa, we can't take her home with us. Let me take her back. I'll say I found her crying in the street. They'll never know I was there."

He snorted, and Hannah's voice rose higher. "We can't! I'm sorry about the bag, all right, but it was too – everything was happening at once, and the dog – the dog was bad enough but you can't kidnap a child! She's just a baby."

Pa bent down and lifted the child, resting her against his shoulder. He began walking away, down the alley towards the light on the main road. The little girl peered over his shoulder, and Hannah saw the whiteness of her face, and the muted terror in her huge dark eyes.

She ran after them. "Pa, you can't do this! I – I won't let you." Even as she said the words, she knew how foolish and weak they sounded. "Pa!" It came out almost as a scream.

Pa whirled around. His hand flew out and slapped her cheek. Her eyes filled with tears, and she tasted blood on her tongue. He grabbed a fistful of her hair and dragged her close to him. His voice was a low growl in the dark. "I am getting very tired of you trying to order me about, my girl. You get no say in this. All you've done is make a mess of things, and you got no right telling me what I can't do. Get that through your stupid thick head."

He released her hair and shoved her away from him.

Hannah closed her eyes, feeling the tears spill over and fall down her cheeks. She took a deep breath. Then she straightened her shoulders, lifted her chin, and followed Pa down the dark alleyway back to where the street was filled with light.

The journey back to their room seemed to go on for hours. Hannah plodded on behind Pa, working hard on putting one foot in front of the other, trying not to think about anything except the scrape of her boots on the cobbles. She glanced up once and met the little girl's wide terrified gaze. She looked away quickly. Her head hurt, and her ear was throbbing. She'd bitten down on the inside of her mouth, and she kept prodding the sore spot with her tongue, tasting the tang of blood and feeling the raw edge of skin.

It was still dark when they did get back home. Hannah kept expecting the sun to have risen, or for it at least to start getting lighter. But the whole event had only taken a few hours, and the sky was still pitch black.

Pa climbed the stairs, opened the door, and dumped the little girl down on the floor. She stumbled to her feet and tried to stagger away from him, but she tripped over her own feet and fell down with a thud. She opened her mouth and let out a loud wail.

"Oh no you don't." Pa dived for her and clapped a hand over her mouth. "Remember what I said?" He caught her plump little hand, and slapped it hard. "You're going to be quiet." He dragged her over to the bed, and dumped her down on the mattress, and threw one of the blankets over her. "Shut your noise."

The little girl struggled for a moment in the blanket's heavy folds, then she lay still, whimpering.

Pa pulled the blanket down from her face. "There," he said, and pulled her up to a sitting position. "Remember what I said. If you're a good girl, then nothing bad will happen."

The little girl nodded. She pulled up handfuls of the rough blanket and pressed them against her face. She shoved a thumb in her mouth and her small round shoulders shook once.

Pa patted her on the head. "Good girl," he said, and stood up. He went to the cupboard and started searching around. "Hannah, where's that bottle, did you move it?"

Hannah was still standing in the doorway. She couldn't tear her gaze away from the tiny shape in the blankets, the desolate droop of the small head, the shudders that kept running through it. The curl papers looked ridiculous now, like a stupid joke that had fallen flat. They didn't belong in a room like this. They belonged in a warm nursery with a nanny, and a mother, and people who cared about whether you were clean and nicely dressed.

There was a lump in Hannah's throat. She wished she could cry again, but all she could feel now was a leaden kind of tiredness.

"Hannah!"

"No, Pa," she said. "I ain't touched your bottle."

Pa growled and grumbled, and banged the kettle and bowls about for a little while longer. "What are you standing there for," he snapped. "Sit down, for goodness sake."

Hannah moved slowly to the stool and sat down. She began to unpick her bootlaces.

Had it only been yesterday she'd sat here and tried to do this exact same thing? Pa had comforted her then, and she'd had the stupid, stupid thought that everything would be all right. Now it was like she didn't know who he was anymore.

"She ain't sleeping in my bed," Pa said. He sat down on the bed, and gave the little girl a shove. "Oi. You. Move along. You going to sleep with Hannah."

The little girl stared at him mutely.

"Go on," he said, and gave her another push. She crawled away from him to the end of the bed. He stood up, grabbed her hand and pulled her off the bed, and dumped her down on Hannah's little tick mattress. "You stay here."

The little girl sat motionless where Pa had put her.

Pa kicked off his boots and pulled the blankets over himself. "You watch her," he said to Hannah. "If she makes any noise, you'll be the one with a thick ear, you understand me?"

"Yes, Pa," Hannah said.

Pa rolled over, and there was silence in the room.

Hannah worked her laces free, and pulled off her boots. She placed them neatly by the door. She took off her shawl and hung it up on its hook.

Within minutes, Pa was snoring loudly.

Hannah stared out of the window, feeling the chill night air creep up her legs. Goosebumps broke out on her arms as she stared up at the dark sky. She couldn't tell for sure, but it looked like the sky was beginning to lighten a little. She must be imagining it. It was still too early for the sunrise.

The little girl hadn't moved. Her bare feet dangled over the edge of the mattress, and she was staring straight ahead of her, as though she were too scared to even look to the side.

Hannah's heart was beating very fast. She couldn't do it. She couldn't go to bed, and lie there with the little girl whom they had just kidnapped from her home. Doing that would mean that this was really happening. If she just stayed at the window and didn't move, then maybe something different would happen. Maybe some answer would present itself.

The little girl didn't move.

Pa turned over and made a snuffling sound. He half woke, sneezed, and then the room was silent again.

Hannah's toes felt stiff. She flexed her fingers, feeling the chill settling into her joints.

Don't stand there like a puppet, Ma would have said, *you'll catch your death of cold*.

Hannah let out her breath in a heart-wrenching sob. She wrapped her arms around her body. She braced herself, and went over to the bed.

The little girl didn't move her head, but her dark eyes darted up for a second before returning to stare blankly in front of her. Hannah sat down on the mattress. Her weight made the little girl slide down towards her, and she let out a tiny noise and threw out her arms trying to steady herself, but immediately after she cowered down, burying her forehead into her knees.

"Hey," Hannah whispered. "It's all right." She put her hand on the little girl's shoulder, but she cringed away from the touch like a frightened dog. Hannah withdrew her hand. What could she do now?

"My name is Hannah," she whispered. "What's your name?"

The little girl said nothing. She didn't even raise her head.

Hannah sighed. She rested her back against the wall and tried to massage some of the tension out of her shoulders. She closed her eyes and stared into the black void behind her eyelids. She felt very tired.

"I'm sorry," she whispered. "I'm so sorry. I didn't mean for any of this to happen. It wasn't how I thought tonight would go. I don't think it's how *he* meant for it to go either, but...

I'm just so sorry. I won't let him hurt you. And I'll try and get you back home as soon as I can."

The little girl stayed silent and motionless.

Hannah took one of the blankets and draped it over the little girl's shoulders. She lay down herself, and stared at the little girl's bent over back. The small tender knobs of her spine showed through the thin fabric of her nightdress.

"I'm so sorry," Hannah whispered.

6

Hannah's dreams were black and sad. She kept seeing the dog again, saw its wiry tail wagging hesitantly, saw its bright eyes gazing up at her, saw its broken body lying motionless on the kitchen floor.

Pa, she cried silently, but Pa wouldn't stop kicking at it.

Then the dog changed into Margaret, and Hannah screamed.

Now you shut up, my girl, Pa said, but it wasn't Pa, it was the young gentleman. *I know you*, he said and blew smoke into her face.

Hands tugged at her dress. Margaret's hands. The little girl's hands. Pa's hands.

A dark alleyway where the young gentleman stood laughing at her, the little girl in his arms, and the dog crushed and bloody underneath his fine heel.

Hannah screamed, but no sound came out. The darkness swept over her and swallowed her.

IN THE MORNING, HANNAH AWOKE TO SOMETHING digging into her throat. The little girl had crept close to her in the night and was now fast asleep, her back against Hannah's stomach and her head underneath Hannah's chin. It was one of her curl papers that had stabbed her.

Hannah stretched cautiously and lay still for a moment, listening. Pa was still snoring. The little girl's breath was shallow and fast. She twitched occasionally, and her little hands opened and closed. Hannah didn't know what to do to comfort her. She tried stroking her forehead, but the little girl frowned in her sleep and let out a tiny cry.

Pa grumbled and snorted. "Wha'?"

"Shh," Hannah whispered in the little girl's ear.

"Mama!" the little girl cried suddenly, waking up all at once. She sat up so suddenly she bumped her head against Hannah's chin, then started once she realised where she was.

"It's all right," Hannah said, reaching for her, but the child flinched away and toppled off the bed. She sat on the floor, gasping, her mouth opening and closing in silent terror.

"It's all right." Hannah followed her off the bed and knelt down, one hand stretched out. She thought for a moment of the dog last night, and quickly squashed the memory. She kept her voice low and comforting. "Do you remember? You came here last night. My name is Hannah, do you remember that?"

The little girl nodded once. She was trembling. "Want my mama," she whispered.

"I know, I know, I'm so sorry. We're going to get you back to your mama as soon as we can. What's your name? Can you tell me your name?"

"Agnes," she whispered.

"Agnes," Hannah repeated. She made herself smile, and hoped it didn't look like a grimace. "What a pretty name. Do you want some breakfast, Agnes?"

The little girl nodded once, slowly.

"Good, that's good, I'll get you something nice. Do you want to come and sit back on the bed? It's so cold on the floor."

Agnes hesitated, and then slowly she stood up. Keeping her eyes on Hannah's face all the while, she stepped carefully over to the bed and climbed back onto the mattress. "Please may I have some kedgeree," she said in a very small, very polite voice.

Hannah suddenly felt like crying. "I'm so sorry, we don't have any kedgeree." What was kedgeree? Was that fish? "We have bread, and I can make toast, and this evening maybe we can have a bit of fried fish, if you would like that. Would you like that?"

Agnes hugged her knees into her chest, and didn't say anything.

Hannah stood up, and realised that Pa was awake, and watching them both.

"Fried fish," he said scornfully. "And who's going to be paying for that, I'd like to know?"

"You want her to starve?" Hannah almost didn't recognise her voice, it sounded so cold and brittle. "We got to give her something, and we've no food in the house, so it might as well be something she'll like."

"Oh, we are high and mighty this morning." Pa yawned, and turned over.

A wave of fury rose up and crashed over Hannah, shocking her with its suddenness and violence. She pressed her cold hands to her hot cheeks, and tried to steady her breath.

Agnes was watching her. Hannah made herself smile. "There, it's all right. No need to fret. Let's see about that toast, shall we?"

"WELL THEN," PA SAID THROUGH A MOUTHFUL OF TOAST.
"When are you heading out?"

Hannah stared at him. "What?"

"You heard me." He brushed crumbs from his beard. They
bounced on his chest and fell to the floor where Hannah
would no doubt be ordered to sweep later on. "Ain't no place
in this world for idle folk. You're going back to your basket."

"No! Pa, you said – "

"I said you didn't have to be a flower girl any more if you
helped me and worked with me. And as I recall, you made a
complete pig's ear of what I asked you to do, and now we
have no money, and a kiddie who's liable to go off at a
moment's notice."

"That's not my fault! You were the one who dragged her
home with us!"

"If you hadn't made such a mess of it all, and maybe actually done what you was told and just picked up that bloody
bag, I wouldn't have needed to drag her at all!" Pa held up his
hand. "Look. I don't want to quarrel. I've said my piece, and I
don't want you sulking or crying about it no more. Things is
what they are. You clearly ain't cut out for my line of business, so you're going back to work with what you do know."

"No, Pa, please..." Hannah's voice was trembling, and she
hated herself for it, but she couldn't stop the burn of tears
threatening to spill over. "At least let me take Agnes home
first."

"No! And I said no crying or whining." His voice was hard
and unyielding as flint. "That's the end of it. If you carry on
whinging like a baby, you'll get the back of my hand. You
understand me, my girl?"

Hannah swallowed furiously. She gave a jerky nod.

"Good. The nipper and I will stay in while I work out how

best to get word to her parents. And then, who knows." He actually smiled. "If they pay up enough, you might not need to go out so much." He leaned across and touched her hand lightly, and now his voice was much softer. "We could maybe get a little cart, a hand cart thing like Simeon down the road has. You could sell baked potatoes, or sandwiches, or hot coffee."

"Soup," Hannah whispered. "I'm good with soup."

"That you are. Sure, that's it, then. Soon as they pay up, we'll get you a little cart and you can peddle hot soup, and maybe some rolls. What do you think?" Pa's voice was soft, and his eyes were kind. He smiled at her, and squeezed her hand. "I know I can be a bit rough. It ain't easy with your ma gone, and I know I got a temper on me. This could be a new start for us both. You and your cart, getting us a steady wage. We might even be able to move somewhere nicer, somewhere it ain't so cramped and we ain't in each other's pockets all the time, and that'll make things easier."

Hannah couldn't stop the tears that spilled down her cheeks. "I – I'd like that, Pa. I'd like that a lot."

"Good." He squeezed her hand again. "That's my girl. See, it'll all work out if you heed what I say."

Hannah nodded, feeling like she was about to choke.

"Good girl. Now." He patted her shoulder. "You get yourself ready to head out. Don't forget to wash your face. And remember, if you don't act like a slattern they won't treat you like a slattern."

Hannah's smile faltered. She glanced at Agnes, who was staring at her with huge scared eyes.

"Go on," Pa said.

Hannah slowly rose and tidied away the plates. Pa got up and went back to lie on the bed, but Agnes stayed perfectly still on the little stool. Only her eyes moved, following Hannah's every movement about the room as she wiped down the table, fastened up her boots, pinned on her bonnet, and wound her shawl around her shoulders.

Hannah hesitated a moment by the door, then went and knelt down by the little stool. "You'll be all right," she told Agnes. "You be a good girl, and mind what Pa tells you."

The little girl's eyes seemed to grow even bigger. "Don't go," she whispered.

Hannah's heart clenched within her. "I'm sorry." She squeezed Agnes' shoulder. "I'll be back soon. I promise."

She stood up and, before she could change her mind, she left the house.

7

Hannah was distracted and silent that day. She walked with Margaret feeling as though she were walking through a strange cloud that distanced her from everything around her. She heard Margaret's shrill little voice rising through the street noise, she felt her feet growing tired in her heavy boots, she felt the sun touch her cheek and warm her body. But all of it seemed to be happening through a filter, as though she were draped in a strange numbing cloth designed to keep the rest of the world at bay.

"Hannah," Margaret said.

"Mm – yeah?"

Margaret sighed. "I said, look at that puppy."

Hannah followed the direction of Margaret's pointing finger, and saw a small white terrier running after a donkey cart. The cart was fresh from Billingsgate, and full of herrings – so full that when the wheel ran over a loose cobble, a couple of fish spilled over the side, and the dog leaped for them. It caught the fish in its jaws, and sat down to eat them in the middle of the road, completely heedless of the road traffic streaming to and fro around it. As soon as it finished tearing the fish to pieces, it scampered after the cart again, waiting for another fish to fall so it could begin the process all over again.

The sight was so comically endearing that Hannah laughed. Margaret laughed too, and for a moment everything felt real.

Then, like a slap in the face, everything hit Hannah again. The dog. Agnes screaming. Shouts upstairs. The dog's wet nose in her palm. Its eager whine. Its panicked bark. Its cries of pain as Pa's boot landed in its side.

"Hannah?" Margaret cried in alarm as she saw the older girl's face turn pale.

"I'm all right," Hannah tried to say, but the words caught in her throat and choked her. She covered her face with her hands and burst into tears.

She was dimly aware of Margaret taking her hand and leading her to a nearby doorway. Margaret sat down on the step next to her, and Hannah buried her head in her arms, and she wept.

How much crying had she done in the last few days, she scolded herself. Why was she acting like this? She wasn't a baby any more.

No, Agnes was a baby. Agnes was a tiny scared child who needed to go home.

"Hannah?" Margaret's voice clung to her, scared and needing reassurance. Hannah felt like screaming. It wasn't Margaret's fault. But right then she didn't feel like she had any reassurance to give. She felt wrung out, squeezed dry by everyone around her. She had to be strong for Margaret, she had to be kind and gentle for Agnes, she had to be strong and smart and silent for Pa, and every day it seemed to be getting harder and harder. No one was being strong or kind for her. She gave, and people took from her, and no one gave anything back.

She wanted Ma, she realised. She wanted someone to give her a hug and tell her it was all going to turn out all right, like Ma used to do. Ma was the one who used to give her courage, who would give her the strength to be kind and smart and patient. She wanted Ma. She needed Ma.

But Ma was dead.

Hannah thought she'd cried out all her tears for Ma already, but it turned out she still had some left.

Pa would never be Ma. He would never be able to support her or help her like Ma had done. If Hannah was a nice person at all now, it was only because of what Ma had given her, and what Ma had taught her. It didn't matter if Pa hugged her or promised her hand carts. Pa was not a good person. He wasn't even a nice person; and Hannah realised suddenly that she did not like Pa at all. Maybe she still loved him in a way – he was her Pa, after all, and she couldn't help that – but she didn't like him. He wasn't the kind of person who she wanted to spend time with, or live with, or even listen to.

She didn't want a soup cart if it meant he'd bought it with money from holding a child to ransom. She didn't want anything more from him. She couldn't stay with him. This wasn't the kind of life Ma would have wanted for her, and it wasn't the kind of life that she wanted for herself, either.

Her savings weren't enough to buy a cart, but they were enough to pay for a bed for a while until she found a job. A real job. A proper job.

Perhaps she could apply to be a baker's apprentice. She couldn't work at the shop close to Pa though. She would have to look for a baker's shop in another part of the City. Somewhere they did not know her. Where she could be respectable.

She would sell her basket, and maybe the Evanses would give her a little food to last her a week or so until she found something. She would be sad to bid the neighbours goodbye. But she had to leave. She couldn't stay with Pa anymore.

Hannah wiped her eyes on her wrist, and fumbled in her sleeve for her handkerchief. She blew her nose, and cleared her throat.

"Hannah," Margaret said. Margaret looked as though she were about to burst into tears herself; her cheeks were very pink, and there was a trail of snot beginning to grow underneath her nose.

Hannah leaned over and put an arm around her. "It's all right. I'm sorry." She laughed wearily. "It's been quite a week."

Margaret scrubbed her nose on her sleeve. "Is it because of that gent yesterday?"

Hannah thought back to that awful encounter, the man's sneering look, his delight at her fear and horror. Was it really just yesterday? So much had happened since then. She gave a little shudder, and hugged Margaret closer.

"No. Well, a little bit. It's not just him. He made me realise some things, I think."

Margaret peered up at her, her brow creased. "I don't understand."

Hannah dropped a kiss on Margaret's forehead. She sighed, and screwed up her courage. "I have to tell you a secret and you have to promise not to tell a soul."

The younger girl stared at her wide-eyed and nodded her consent to keep the confidence.

"I'm going away soon, Margaret. I need to. I have to find somewhere else to live, and I can't be a flower girl anymore. I'm too old, and − and you need to be careful in this job. I'm going to have a word with Kitty, you know the girl from the stall in Covent Garden? I'll see if she can sort out someone else for you to walk with. But − " Hannah hesitated, then plunged on. "You need to start thinking about doing something else too, Margaret. It isn't safe for you."

"What?" Margaret asked, as Hannah had known she would. "Why? What do you mean, it ain't safe?"

"That gent the other day. He... he thought I was doing something else. He thought I was someone else. And as you get older, you find more and more people – more men – they start to think you're something else when you're not."

"I don't understand." Margaret was shaking her head. "I don't understand. Why are you going?"

Hannah took a deep breath. "All right. I'm going to explain it all. You got to listen really carefully. This is very important."

Margaret listened with varying reactions of disgust, shock, and incredulity. "That ain't right," she said more than once. "You're having me on."

"No, I'm not," Hannah said. "Now shush and listen." She explained for another several minutes. "Right," she said finally. "Does that all make sense?"

Margaret was silent for a while, thinking it all over. Eventually she nodded her head. "I s'pose."

"Good." Hannah blew out her breath in a long sigh.

"Did your ma tell you all this?" Margaret said.

"A bit. But most of the important stuff I heard from the other girls."

Margaret nodded slowly. Her round little face was very grave, and Hannah felt a sudden pang. This was how it started. This was the beginning of the end of Margaret's childhood. There wasn't any way back from this knowledge, and everything that it meant. But it was better to know. Margaret couldn't have stayed a child forever.

"You promise me you'll be careful," Hannah said. She stood up, and pulled Margaret to her in a tight crushing hug. "You be so careful," she whispered into her hair. "Not just about *that*. But be careful with your life. Make sure it's the one you want, and not one that someone else is making you live. You always got a choice, you remember that. It doesn't matter if it's about a man, or about whatever."

Margaret squeezed her hard. "I will." She wriggled back and looked up at her. "You're really going?"

Hannah nodded.

8

As Hannah climbed the stairs up to the house door, she could hear the Evans children below playing and shouting with each other. She heard Mrs Evans yelling at them all to be quiet, and then something else in Welsh she didn't understand. She paused for a moment, her hand on the rickety rail, and listened to the cheerful noise and hubbub. It was so different to the sour silence she so often had to endure with Pa, and she wondered why she'd never noticed it before, or thought to do anything about it.

Well, she was making changes now.

She squared her shoulders and lifted her chin, and marched up the stairs. Inside the room was cold and dark. Pa hadn't lit the lamp, and when she heard the rising rasp of his snore, she knew why.

Agnes had moved from the chair where Hannah had left her, and was now sitting on the little mattress, the blankets wrapped around her body with only her head poking out. She shrank back against the wall when Hannah entered, huddling even deeper in the nest of bedclothes until only her eyes showed, watching Hannah with fearful intensity.

Hannah hung up her shawl and bonnet, then approached the bed with an outstretched hand.

Agnes drew back at first, but when Hannah smiled at her, she hesitantly let the blankets fall from around her mouth so Hannah could see her offering up a shy, wary half-smile in return.

Hannah beamed. "There's a good girl. Now, what about some dinner? I got some fried fish, would you like some fish?"

Agnes nodded, and Hannah set about in the kitchen, unwrapping the paper parcel under her arm. The fish had cooled on her journey home, but she laid it out on the rough wooden platter, which she placed on the table along with a heavy bottle of gin.

She beckoned Agnes to come and sit down. Agnes slid quietly off the bed out of the little nest of blankets, and crept over to the little stool where she had sat before.

"Pa," Hannah called.

Pa's snores paused for a moment, then started again.

"Pa!" she said again, more loudly, and he grunted and turned over.

"Wha'."

"Pa, dinner's ready."

He groaned, and heaved himself up and lumbered over to the table. He sat down, eyed the bottle of gin hungrily, then stared down at the platter. "What's this, then."

"Fish."

"Why've we got fish?"

"It's for Agnes."

"Agnes?" Pa stared blankly for a moment, then looked at Agnes, who shrank away before his gaze. "Oh." He was groggy but the memory of why the child was there was gradually coming back to him.

Hannah ignored him, and set to cutting up one of the

pieces of fish for Agnes. Agnes carefully tried a mouthful, chewing with a puzzled expression on her face.

"Fish," Pa said scornfully. "No call for you to be wasting money on damn fish."

"Isn't stopping you eating it, though, is it," Hannah retorted.

Pa looked surprised for a second, then frowned. "Who spit in your porridge, young miss?"

"No one. You just don't need to moan and complain all the time, is all."

"Moaning?" A dangerous note crept into Pa's voice. "I won't stand for that kind of cheek, my girl."

Hannah's voice was shaking. "Ma wouldn't have wanted you to be like this."

There was a short sharp silence. Hannah wrapped her hands together in her lap, and stared down at the fish before her. Her breath felt tight and fast in her chest. She could feel Pa staring at the top of her head. From the corner of her eye, she saw Agnes frozen in mid-chew, her little hand clenched around the fork with white bloodless knuckles.

Finally Pa said, "You don't know what your ma would or wouldn't have wanted."

"I know it's not this." Hannah's throat ached. She wouldn't cry. Not anymore.

Pa grunted, and took a mouthful of fish. He carried on eating, and eventually so did Hannah, though every muscle in her body felt strung tight with anxious nerves.

"Sent the note," he said as Hannah started clearing the table. He jerked his head towards Agnes. "To her folks."

Hannah's heart gave a sudden jolt. "When?"

"This afternoon. Gave 'em two days to get their savings together."

"And what if they don't have the money?"

Pa shrugged. "They will. Fancy grocer in his big house. He'll have more than enough."

Hannah had an idea and she knew she would have to approach Pa as nonchalant as possible if it was to work.

"While we wait for the ransom, why don't I take Agnes with me to sell flowers," she said.

Pa eyed her like she had suggested she pay a visit to the royal family. "No." He returned his gaze to his plate of food, signaling the discussion was over.

Hannah drew in a deep breath. "We could sell so many more flowers if she were along, Pa."

His head jolted up, eyes black, "Are you back-talking again?"

"No, but just listen. Please." Hannah's courage surprised herself as much as her father. "I hardly sold anything today. I told you the customers aren't as eager to buy from an older girl. Look at her. Look at her face. Her eyes. I know I could make more money if Agnes was with me." She held Pa's gaze with confidence before daring to add, "She trusts me."

After a long pause, Pa said, "All right. But I want you right home at the regular time. And you better earn double what you did today."

He yawned and stretched, then grabbed the bottle of gin and went back to bed.

Hannah finished clearing up, and then dragged the chair to the window and sat down, gazing out at the sky above. It was still light, but streaks of yellow and orange were beginning to smear up behind the houses.

Not long now.

She pressed her hands against her mouth, smelling the greasy fish on her fingers. A hard tight knot of fear began to twist behind her breastbone, and all her earlier courage felt small and thin and weak. It wasn't enough. She wasn't enough. The world was too big for her. So many people tried and failed to make their own lives out there. There wasn't anything about Hannah that was any different to them. It was mad to think she could succeed where so many others failed.

There was a rustle and a soft step, and when Hannah looked around, Agnes was standing next to her.

"Are you all right?" Hannah asked in a low voice.

Agnes nodded once, and then she came and leaned against Hannah's shoulder, looking out with her at the fading sky. "It's pretty," she whispered.

"Yes." Hannah put her arm around her. She closed her eyes and smelled the top of her head. It reminded her of Mrs Evans' Daffyd, and it brought her back a faint scrap of courage. Her heart was still beating uncomfortably fast, but she breathed deep, and drew Agnes onto her lap. Agnes rested against her, the top of her head trying to fit underneath Hannah's chin.

Hannah laughed. "Shall we take these curl papers out? They keep on stabbing me."

Agnes nodded solemnly, and sat very still while Hannah started unwrapping the papers and knots from the little girl's head. There were fourteen in total, and many of them were already beginning to work themselves loose.

Agnes' hair came down in a heavy dark tumble of waves and tight bunched-up tangles. Hannah tried to comb them out with her fingers, but she hit a knot almost at once.

While Hannah was picking it out with her nails, Agnes said, "Mama does it with a comb."

"What does she do, my sweet?"

"My hair. She makes my curls with a comb."

Hannah's fingers stilled in Agnes' hair. For a moment she was silent, gazing down at the pure white line of the little girl's scalp where it showed through her heavy dark hair.

Then she squeezed Agnes' shoulders and whispered, "You'll see your mama soon."

Agnes' head drooped. She didn't say anything, and Hannah felt the heaviness of guilt drop into her stomach.

"Soon," she whispered into the top of Agnes' head.

Agnes stayed silent, and Hannah went back to working the tangles out of her hair. She glanced over her shoulder, and thought she saw Pa staring at them. But the shadows were thickening, and she couldn't tell if it was just her mind playing tricks.

৩৯৪

PA FINISHED THE BOTTLE BY THE TIME THE SUN WENT down. Hannah waited until the room was dark, and the only sounds were Pa's snores and the soft sigh of Agnes' breath as she lay fast asleep, still nestled into Hannah's breast.

Hannah stared at the dark sky. She had no way of telling the time, but it must have been an hour since sunset. She knew she needed to sleep, to gather her strength for the days ahead. Her heart pounded so hard she was certain she could hear it, that it would wake Pa.

It felt as if she lay awake for hours listening to Pa snore and Agnes whimper, but she eventually fell into a fitful sleep.

When she heard the far off cries of a costermonger, she jolted awake. The first glimpse of daylight was visible and she feared she had overslept and missed her opportunity.

Hannah lay still, listening for a moment, then relaxed when she recognised the steady, laboured breathing that meant Pa was still in a deep sleep. She rubbed Agnes gently on her back and quickly motioned for her to remain silent but to get up and put her shoes on.

She felt along the wall for the loose brick, and eased it out enough to put her hand into the small space. Her fingers touched the hidden purse, and she quickly tucked it away in her stays. She took one of the blankets from the bed, and made up a bundle with the kitchen knife, the kettle, her hair-pins, and a spare pair of stockings. She put the bundle into her flower basket, tied on her shawl, pinned on her bonnet, and silently tip-toed towards the door.

With the basket handle looped over one arm, Hannah reached her other hand out to Agnes, who grasped it and followed her to the door, silently, as if sensing the need to be stealthy.

Hannah opened the door carefully and gulped in the cool, damp air before inching onto the rickety wooden landing.

"Where the hell are you sneaking off to, girl!"

9

Hannah gasped and nearly jumped out of her shoes. Agnes started to cry as she grabbed onto Hannah's legs.

"Pa," she said with more calm than she felt. "I didn't mean to wake you."

"I'll bet you didn't." He lumbered towards the door as he dragged his trousers up to his waist and buckled his belt.

"The costermonger woke me so I thought it best to get started selling flowers early, while the business men are heading to work in the City." She swallowed hard, hoping she had sounded convincing.

"I'll go along as well," said Pa. "Just to make sure our little treasure hear stays safe."

Hannah's shoulders sagged and she fought to withhold a deep sigh. "We'll never sell anything with you standing by, Pa."

"I'll stay out of sight. Won't no one but you know I'm there." He sneered at her with a knowing smile as he closed the door to their room behind him and followed the two girls from the alley onto the high street.

❦

HANNAH WAS BESIDE HERSELF WITH DESPERATION. WITH Pa watching her every move from around the corner, she was so nervous she could barely approach the fine ladies and gentlemen who walked past her. Each time they shook their heads and quickened their pace to be away from her, Hannah would look up and see Pa scowling. Sometimes he would motion with his hand, pointing his finger first to his eye and then at her to let her know that nothing was escaping his attention.

Luckily, several of the women and a few of the men to whom she would say, "*sweet violets*" as she held a bunch in their direction did stop. They would look from her to Agnes and back again, a sadness in their eyes when they assumed the two girls were sisters and homeless. In their unmasked distress to see the dirty and disheveled younger girl, eyes wide and cheeks tear-stained, they bought bunches of flowers. Many bunches.

That evening, Pa was clearly pleased with the amount of coins she deposited on the table.

"Looks as if you aren't such a bad business woman after all, Hannah girl." He laughed loudly as he counted the coins. "Maybe we shouldn't give the little one back, even when they do pay."

Hannah was horrified. She was also afraid that Pa would notice the bulk at the bottom of her basket that still contained the few items she had packed that morning. Or that he would notice the items missing from their usual place. She only had one more day before the ransom was due to sneak away with Agnes and take her home. Her mind was turning over a thousand ideas when Pa presented the opportunity she needed.

"I've got somewhere to be tomorrow," he said. "You go

back and do the same thing like you did today. But don't take your eyes off the little one, you hear."

"Yes, Pa." Hannah did not look at him, but continued to prepare the sausage and biscuits that they'd purchased for dinner on their way home. Even Pa was in such a good mood from their earnings that he was happy to indulge.

⁂

"VIOLETS, MISS?" AGNES STARED AT THE COUNTESS WITH wide, imploring eyes as she boldly stepped forward from her usual place hidden behind Hannah's skirt. It distressed Hannah to see how quickly the girl had adapted to the life-style she had been thrust into after only two days. It was as if Agnes knew that her very life depended on it.

The Countess quickly averted her eyes from the two obviously poor urchins. She opened her silk purse to withdraw several coins and handed them to her lady's maid. "Clara, purchase a bunch of violets from the child."

Clara counted the coins she had been given and looked at her mistress in bewilderment. "My lady, this is far more than it cost for a week's worth of violets."

The Countess flashed a look of disapproval at Clara, clearly unhappy by the maid's questioning of her intentions. It was unnecessary for the titled woman to say another word.

"Yes, my lady." Clara lowered her head and handed the coins to Hannah, assuming the older girl handled the money, and accepted the proffered bundle of violets from Agnes. After the exchange, Clara scrambled to climb into the carriage behind her mistress.

As the footman clicked his tongue to urge the horses forward, Hannah made a split second decision. She grabbed Agnes by the hand and dragged her to the side of the carriage, lifting her onto the frame at the back of the enclo-sure, out of sight of the footman and the passengers.

"Grab on," she urged, as she jumped onto the carriage as well just before it picked up speed and rounded the corner.

Hannah was certain that the carriage was travelling in the direction of Marylebone where Agnes lived. As soon as she saw the familiar row of houses where they'd kidnapped Agnes, they would leap from the carriage and Hannah would see Agnes safely home before heading off on her own journey. The coins she had received from the Countess would be enough for food for several days if she was careful.

It was difficult to hang on as the carriage lurched and bounced on the uneven cobblestones. Hannah had to wrap herself around Agnes as well, who was holding on so tight that her knuckles were white from the exertion. After a good ten minutes of being jostled so roughly that she thought her insides would spill out, the carriage slowed and turned into an archway toward a private residence.

"Jump now, Agnes," Hannah whispered and, before the child had a chance to know what was happening, she pried the girls grip from the carriage, wrapped her arms around her waist, and leapt from the carriage, tumbling them both to the ground.

"Hurry!"

Hannah took Agnes' hand and led her, running back to the high street teeming with pedestrian traffic, where they could slip into a crowd undetected while she got her bearings.

❧

NEARLY AN HOUR AND A HALF HAD PASSED AND HANNAH was distraught. Nothing in the area looked familiar. Agnes did not know her home address and every question Hannah tried to ask her about where she lived caused her more distress to the point that the little girl was so scared she was crying. Hannah had lifted Agnes into her arms to comfort her, and Agnes wrapped her legs around her waist, latching her arms around Hannah's neck, and would not let go.

Hannah was certain she had gone in circles which was confirmed when she recognised one of the roads that they had turned onto while still aboard the carriage. She could do no more than try to trace their journey backwards and start over from a point of familiarity. She was exhausted from carrying Agnes but did not feel she could put the child down, her head lolling to one side and resting on Hannah's shoulder.

She stopped at a corner, indecision between which direction to turn allowing her to drop her guard, when a heavy hand dropped onto her shoulder and roughly gathered up the neckline of her dress, yanking her backwards and nearly choking her.

Agnes stirred and woke, bumping her head against Hannah's cheek. She screamed as she recognised their assailant. Hannah began to turn around, but Pa was too fast. He slapped her cheek before she could defend herself, her arms still wrapped around Agnes.

"Bloody hell!" he roared, "what do you think you're doing, you stupid girl!"

"Pa, no! Stop!" She let Agnes slip out of her arms and placed her gently on the ground on her feet. Agnes hid behind her and held onto her skirt.

"How dare you defy me!"

"It isn't what you think," she cried. "We've done so well today. Look!"

Hannah dug into her pocket and withdrew the coins from the Countess, holding them in the palm of her hand towards her father. He roughly grabbed them, nearly taking her hand with them, and shoved them deep into his own dirty trouser pocket.

"Where have you been?" He was still breathing heavy but his voice was coming into control.

"We weren't selling so much in our regular place today, so we went around the corner." Hannah took a deep breath and steadied her voice. She had to convince Pa that she wasn't trying to escape. Her life, and Agnes', depended on it. "There were so many people and we just kept walking along and selling violets. I lost track of how far we went."

Pa looked at her, his eyebrow raised, with a skeptical gaze. "Let's get home. We'll buy some bacon and cheese for dinner."

Hannah thought she could almost see the hint of a smile on his lips and was grateful for the generosity of the Countess, although felt a stab in the pit of her stomach at having lost the small fortune that would have given her a good start out on her own.

HANNAH AWOKE TO THE SOUND OF PUSHCARTS ROLLING down the alley outside of their room and knew that she had slept later than normal. After yesterday's close call with Pa, she was not going to chance another early departure. If she raised his suspicions again, she had no plausible explanations left to tell him.

She hoped that after the significant earnings that she and Agnes had brought back the previous day, he would leave them on their own again today. She only needed one more day and she was certain she could spirit Agnes back to her home.

One more day.

She rose from her bed and pulled the blankets back up around Agnes' chin, allowing her a few extra minutes of sleep before she would wake the exhausted child. She poured water from a pitcher into a bowl and soaked a wash cloth in the cool liquid, wrung it out and wiped the sleep from her eyes.

As she laced her shoes and prepared to wake Agnes, Hannah realised that Pa was staring at her. She returned his gaze tentatively, but said nothing.

"I've got an errand for you today," he said, his voice gruff from last night's whiskey and sleep. "You're going to pick up the ransom money." He pointed to the sleeping bundle on Hannah's mattress. "*She* stays with me."

❧ 10 ❧

Hannah's stomach clenched. Surely he was not expecting her to carry out his criminal deed. She was planning to see Agnes safely delivered home today and put an end to this nonsense. What if she were caught?

"But, Pa -," she started.

"Shut your mouth, girl," he barked. "It's an easy pick up. The money will be in a brown wrapper around the side of St. Pauls Church in Covent Garden, hidden in a trash bin. All you have to do is walk to the church with your basket of flowers, offer some to the people out front, and then slip around the side and find the package. It's easier for you to do it than me. No one will be looking for a young girl."

Hannah saw the resolve in his eyes and knew he would not be dissuaded from sending her on this unfortunate mission. If only Agnes could go with her, she could still carry out her plan and slip away.

"I could sell more flowers with Agnes along," she said, biting her lip as she waited hopefully for a response.

"Too dangerous. Someone from her house might be lurking about after dropping off the ransom."

At least if Hannah came home with the ransom, she'd be able to return Agnes to her home. Then Hannah could worry about how and when she would make her own escape. Her resolve was strong now, and she would find a way. First things first, and seeing Agnes returned safely home was number one.

HANNAH APPROACHED THE FRONT OF THE MODEST STONE church in Bedford Street with trepidation. She clenched the handle of her flower basket with a sweaty hand, still acutely aware of the items tucked underneath the violets that she took from the kitchen for her planned flight less than 48 hours earlier. It felt like weeks had passed since she had helped Pa break into the house in Marylebone and they'd brought Agnes home.

There were more than a dozen people lingering in the square closest to the large columns supporting the portico at the entrance to St. Pauls Church near Covent Garden market. Most of the pedestrians were on their way to or from the market and seemed to take a moment near the church to pause and catch their breath a bit removed from the hectic atmosphere and chaos of the marketplace.

"Lovely violets," Hannah said, although her voice was so timid that no one took notice. She tried to appear natural and prayed that none of the passersby would pay her the least bit of attention as she strolled in the square by the church.

When she felt that no one was paying her any mind, she sauntered casually along one side of the stone wall and saw the bin that Pa described. If she was lucky, the package with the ransom money would be easily retrieved and she would be on her way home in a few minutes.

Her heart pounded in her chest as she swung her basket of violets in the way she had seen some of the other girls around the flower stalls do. As she approached the trash bin, she slowed down, her eyes darting from one person to the next. No one was looking her way.

Hannah stopped by the bin and peered into it. She saw scraps of greasy paper that had been wrapped around food, discarded by whoever had eaten its contents. The bin was not very full which meant she would have to stretch down to reach the contents and fish around for the package she was meant to retrieve.

She wrinkled her nose as she caught a whiff of something foul in the bin and forced herself to plunge her hand deep into the fetid debris. With a swift dive as she tried to ignore the slimy food remnants that stuck to her hand, she grasped a package that had the right size and shape of what she was after. She pulled it up, shaking bits of discarded rubbish from the brown wrapper and slipped it into her basket.

"Game's up, missy."

A huge paw of a hand clamped around Hannah's upper arm and yanked her back. She gasped and turned toward the massive uniformed constable that had a hold of her.

"What!? I ... I don't understand," she stammered.

"Where is the girl?"

"What girl?"

"Don't play coy with me." The constable's grip tightened on her arm and she winced in pain.

"I don't know what you're talking about." Hannah was shaking. She had to calm herself. *Think of something.*

"I supposed you plan to tell me you don't know what's in that package you recovered from the trash and hid in your basket?"

"No, I ...,"

"You're a thief and a kidnapper and you're going with me. You know exactly what you came after, don't you?"

Hannah's very existence, her life, would hereafter be determined by how she responded to this question. In a matter of seconds, she imagined being dragged to the police station, held in a cell, taken up before a magistrate, and sent to a workhouse. Or worse. What would become of Agnes? Her father?

"Answer me!" The constable shook her so hard her teeth rattled.

"Sir, I was looking for food," she said. Her eyes welled with tears. "I'm hungry and I did not sell any of my violets today. I saw some food in this bin, and then saw an unopened package that looked like it was discarded by a street vendor. I hoped to find a pickle or even a piece of fish once I unwrapped it."

Hannah stood taller and stared directly into the constable's stern brown eyes. She felt his grip loosen slightly and started to breathe.

"Give it here," he said, holding his hand out for the package.

Hannah dug into her basket and removed the brown paper package, handing it over to him with shaking hands. The constable turned the package over, slipped a finger under the string and loosened it, then unwrapped the contents of the package. He took out the half-inch wad and thumbed through it. Hannah could see it was a wad of plain vellum, cut about the size of banknotes.

It was a trap. The package had been placed to simulate the appearance of the ransom, so that whoever came to collect it would be apprehended by the police.

The constable hesitated, then dug into his pocket and removed a six-pence. He tossed it to Hannah and said, "Here. Buy yourself a meal."

She stood for a moment and looked at the coin in her hand, stunned.

"Go on with you now. Run along."

And she was only too happy to oblige.

❦

PA WAS PACING THE FLOOR WHEN HANNAH FINALLY returned to their room.

"You got it?" He practically pounced on her when she opened the door.

"It wasn't there," she said quickly, wanting to deliver the bad news as fast as possible.

The entire walk home she tried to think through her options. Should she tell her father what happened, that she was nearly apprehended by the constable? If she did, would he let her return Agnes to her home and put an end to this debacle?

Knowing Pa, he would send an even harsher demand to Agnes' family, maybe even threatening her harm if they did not play by his rules. He would be furious to hear that they'd gone to the police and set a trap for his capture.

She would need to convince him that there was a mix-up in days or that they had not had enough time to gather the money and she should try again the next day. If she could persuade him to let Agnes go with her, as a decoy, to help sell flowers while she found the package, perhaps she could escape. Of course, she would not go near the church at Covent Garden but would take Agnes directly home and then disappear herself. If only she still had the money the Countess had given her.

"What do you mean it wasn't there?"

Hannah was now sitting on her mattress with Agnes in her lap. The child did not look worse for the wear for spending the day at home with Pa, but she put her arms around Hannah and hugged her, looking genuinely pleased to see her.

"Are you sure you had the right day? You counted two days from when we brought Agnes home but maybe they are counting two days after they received your demand letter. Maybe they think the day is tomorrow?" Hannah held her breath, hoping her logic was plausible.

Pa hesitated and seemed to be deep in thought as he counted on his fingers.

"I can try again tomorrow," she said.

She pried Agnes' fingers from her waist and left her sitting on the bed as she moved toward the small table where they ate their meals. There was still some cheese left from the previous day's dinner and Hannah had purchased a stale loaf of day-old bread from the baker so she went about preparing their evening meal.

As they ate, Hannah attempted to gain Pa's confidence in her willingness to be part of his plan.

"I did not sell many flowers today. The people at the market did not look kindly on me and stared the whole time. That made it more difficult to check the trash bin discreetly."

Pa grunted as he shovelled bread and cheese into his mouth, eating quickly to be sure he got his fill.

Hannah continued, an animated lilt to her voice. "I think Agnes should be with me tomorrow to sell the flowers. The customers are drawn to her and she will keep people distracted while I collect the package."

Pa looked up at her as he continued chewing, but still did not say a word.

"Whatever we take in from the flower sales will just be a bonus on top of the ransom money," Hannah added before taking a bit of her own bread.

They ate in silence for a few minutes more. Hannah could

practically see Pa consider the pros and cons in his head as he considered her suggestion.

They finished their meal and Hannah cleaned the dishes, then settled with Agnes on the bed. She would miss the child whom she had come to think of as a younger sister in the few short days they had been together.

"Would you like to hear a story," she spoke in a low voice to Agnes so as not to disturb Pa who had moved to his own bed with his whiskey bottle in his fist.

Hannah recited a short fairy tale to Agnes from memory, a story her mother used to tell her in happier days. She wasn't even sure Agnes had heard the ending, realising the child was asleep when she finished.

Pa lumbered from his bed to put the whiskey bottle back on the shelf and blow out the candle that dimly lit the dark room. As he climbed back into bed to go to sleep, Hannah heard his voice in the darkness.

"I'll go myself to pick up the ransom tomorrow. You stay here with the girl until I get back."

Hannah awoke early but pretended she was still asleep. Agnes lay sleeping beside her and Pa was still snoring. If she let Pa go to look for the ransom, he might be arrested. Then again, perhaps the police were no longer surveilling the area because the pick-up date really *was* yesterday. That was just a story she told Pa about miscounting the days to convince him that a mistake had been made.

It would be all right. He would go to St. Paul's Church at Covent Garden and look for the ransom. After a while, he would give up and come home. But she would already be gone, having taken Agnes home and then be on her way somewhere else. Anywhere else.

She would wait until he was gone at least half an hour, then she would leave and wind her way to Marylebone. She was sure she would remember the way from their room to Agnes' house. She only got lost two days ago because she tried to find her way from a different starting point.

Pa stirred. He got out of bed and poured some water into a bowl, splashed his face, and then wiped it with his shirt.

There was still a crust of bread left which he picked up and gnawed on as he moved around the dimly lit room. A stream of sunlight shone through the crack in the wooden shutter in front of the window. It was going to be a hot, humid day.

"I'll be going now." His voice boomed and echoed in the small room, indifferent to whether or not he woke her or Agnes from sleep. "Stay inside today. Keep the girl out of sight."

"Yes, Pa," she said. It was not like Hannah to lie to Pa. She had always obeyed him. But she knew in her heart that what he was doing was wrong. What he had been doing for a long time was wrong.

Agnes stirred beside her and she stroked her hair to comfort her. She didn't dare speak any words to her until Pa was away.

***

THERE WASN'T A CLOUD IN THE SKY AND THE SUN WAS directly overhead, heating the cobblestones around the marketplace to a temperature that could fry eggs. The vendors retreated to the edges of the market to seek the cover of shade from the surrounding buildings. Tired voices beckoned to customers with less enthusiasm than normal as they attempted to hawk their wares.

The heavy set man with the unshaven face and soiled clothes lumbered around the front of St. Paul's Church. He raised his head and gazed up at the massive column holding up the stone portico and marvelled at the architectural miracle that could be achieved. There were few people nearby, the heat frightening most to stay away from the marketplace today.

He wandered around the side of the church and saw the trash bin that he had selected himself a few days earlier when he put his plan into motion. He had suffered long enough. His wife had died an untimely and painful death. He could not provide for his daughter who he had to force onto the street to earn money to feed them both. He was a miserable sod but he could start anew.

He had not hurt the little girl. In fact, Hannah had treated her like a sister and taken good care of her. The grocer had more than enough money that he could afford to share a little with him and Hannah for having taken such good care of his daughter.

All of these thoughts ran through his mind in an attempt to justify his actions as he walked purposefully to the trash bin and reached in, found the thick rectangular package wrapped in brown paper, retrieved it, shoved it in his pocket, and turned to walk away.

He continued to the front of the church square, resisting the temptation to withdraw the package from his pocket and open it. He smiled. It felt right. He was sure everything was going to be all right now. He would stop his thieving ways, buy a hand cart just like he told Hannah, and prove to her that he could provide her with a good life.

❦

It was a long walk to Marylebone. Agnes clutched Hannah's hand the entire time and, from time to time, she asked to be carried, which Hannah was only too happy to oblige. She would miss the child. She thought also of Margaret, who was like a little sister to her, and was both sad and frightened about what lay ahead for her. She wondered if she had thought everything through well enough or if she should return to Pa and try to save up more money before she ventured out on her own.

Pa would be furious with her if he came home to find

Agnes gone. No, she had no choice now. She had made her decision and there was no going back.

As they approached the Marylebone High Street, Agnes lifted her head from Hannah's shoulder.

"Hungry," she said in a weak voice.

Although Hannah was sure they had nearly reached Agnes' home and she wanted to save what little money she had, she also did not want to return Agnes appearing as if she had been starved during her ordeal. She looked around and found a baker's shop about half block away. She hoped she could purchase a small bit of bread that would not be too dear.

The bell jangled as she pushed through the door and she let Agnes slip from her arms. The little girl ran to the glass counter and peered at the sweet treats, her delight and longing perceptible. As if to accentuate her hunger, her belly let out a low rumble.

"May I help you?" A young woman no older than Hannah asked her.

"A penny loaf, please," she asked. She hoped it would be enough to split with Agnes. She was hungry as well and the child would be home soon, so she didn't feel bad about sharing a single portion with her.

The clerk reached for the bread and stretched over the counter to hand it to Hannah, who dug in her purse for a penny.

"Thank you." As she started to turn away and exit the shop, her eye caught a small hand-printed notice on the wall.

Help Wanted.

Hannah stopped. She stared at the sign a moment. Agnes tugged at her skirt and held a hand up for the bread. Without even tearing off a piece for herself, Hannah handed the penny loaf to Agnes, who tucked in with relish.

"Excuse me," Hannah said to the young woman who had

sold her the bread. "I would like to apply for the position." She pointed to the sign.

The clerk looked her up and down. "You'd have to talk to my Ma. She's out delivering right now."

"I can come back," Hannah said eagerly. "In an hour?"

"It's hard work. Up almost all night tending the ovens, then taking the first shift selling in the morning until I can get here. You have to sleep in a room back there." She motioned with her thumb to a heavy wooden door behind her.

A place to sleep.

Hannah could not believe her luck as she excitedly said to the young woman, "I'll be back!"

The girl shook her head in disbelief as Hannah and Agnes exited the shop.

❀

HE LOOKED HEAVENWARD AND WIPED THE SWEAT FROM HIS brow with the sleeve of his shirt. It would be an exhausting walk home in this heat, but he didn't mind. He hadn't felt this good in years. He had not noticed the two uniformed constables watching from behind the columns of the church who were now closing in from behind.

They each grabbed one arm, the officer on the right twisting one up behind his back in a painful, distorted position.

"What the ...,"

"The jig is up, mate," said the one on the left. "Where's the girl?"

His shoulders sagged and he turned his head from one side to the other, evaluating his predicament. A sinking feeling came over him and he slumped to his knee, suddenly overcome with the blistering heat of the sun.

"C'mon man, on your feet. Where is she?"

"She's safe. She's with my daughter."

"Give us the address. You're going to the clink. For a good long time."

It took a while to find the exact street in Marylebone where Hannah and Pa had snatched Agnes. Agnes walked a little bit of the way from the baker's, but before too long she was begging to be carried again, and for the final stretch of the journey she was asleep with her head resting on Hannah's shoulder.

When they approached the street where Agnes' family lived, Hannah woke her and slid her to the sidewalk, then took her hand. This time, she did not turn down the alleyway behind the terrace houses, but headed for the main road where the rows of white and brick homes showcased their welcoming front doors.

Hannah imagined herself arriving at a home like this one day, knocking properly to visit the lady of the house for tea. She hesitated for a moment before she took the step up from the sidewalk to the door.

Agnes was still sleepy and did not appear to realise where she was yet. Hannah brushed a stray lock of hair from the little girl's face.

"Goodbye Agnes," she whispered, and was startled to find tears springing to her eyes as Agnes gazed up at her, clearly bewildered. Hannah bent and placed a quick kiss on the child's forehead, then rang the doorbell. She waited long enough to hear footsteps approaching, then grabbed her basket and ran to the end of the street, ducking down by the fence so she could still see what happened.

The front door opened, and warm yellow light spilled out.

A man's voice cried, "Oh!" and then broke into something like a sob. Hannah saw a young man in a faded blue dressing gown kneel down by Agnes and gather her into his arms. "Oh, my darling girl!"

Another voice came from inside the house, and then a young woman appeared. She almost collapsed down beside them, and burst into tears.

Agnes seemed stunned for a moment, unable to quite comprehend where she was, but then cried, "Mama! Papa!" with such love and joy that Hannah felt a lump tighten in her throat. She watched the three of them huddled together on the step, their arms around each other, their faces bathed with the golden light spilling out around them. She swallowed hard, and felt the tears track hot trails down her cheeks.

Then she hoisted up her basket, and set out in the direction of the baker's shop.

EPILOGUE

TWO YEARS LATER ....

"Hannah!" Mrs Grainger called. "The loaves are done now, be a lamb and let them cool."

Hannah wiped her floury hands on her apron, and left the batch of dough she was kneading. The ovens at the back of the bakery were hot dark monsters, but she loved the smell of fresh bread and pastry that wafted out of them. She took a towel to protect her hands, and slid the tray of fresh-baked loaves out of the oven, setting them down to cool on the side.

"Thanks, pet." Mrs Grainger wiped her broad red forehead with the back of her hand, leaving a white streak of sweaty flour. "Goodness but it's busy today, ain't it? Would you be a duck and serve this gentleman while I wash my hands?"

The bakery always saw a steady stream of customers, but now the weather was on the turn, people were out in droves stocking up on warm bread and hot pastries. Some people had already put in orders for Christmas cake and plum pudding, and one of Mrs Grainger's regular customers was getting married soon and had placed their largest order yet for sweet pastries.

Hannah smiled as she wiped her hands clean and went through to the shop. Sally, the other girl who worked in the bakery, and Hannah's roommate, had been talking about going to the music hall tonight. It was becoming a regular habit for the two of them to take a bag of the leftover pastries that would otherwise be thrown out, and spend an evening at the halls, laughing at the variety acts and gorging themselves on sweet cakes. It made a nice warm feeling in her stomach, anticipating the evening, and she was still smiling when she reached the counter.

"Good morning," she said cheerily, "how can I help?" She looked up at the customer, and the smile died on her face.

Although she had not seen him in two years and he had aged ten, she recognised him immediately.

Pa shifted his weight awkwardly and cleared his throat. "I'll have a currant bun."

Hannah's heart was pounding in her chest. Her Pa was standing right in front of her. A free man.

Six months after she took Agnes home and started her job in the bakery, she'd mustered the courage to visit her's and Pa's old room. He had not been there, nor any of his things. In his place was a young couple with a newborn baby, but they claimed to know nothing about the previous tenant.

Mrs Evans saw her as she was leaving and threw her arms about her. Hannah hugged her former neighbour and friend tightly.

"Oh, child, I've been so fearful of what has become of you. Are you all right? You look well." She said this with surprise, having expected the worst.

"Where is my father?" Hannah asked.

"You don't know?" Mrs Evans had responded.

Hannah shook her head.

"A constable came by here one day about half a year ago. He was asking about you and said he was also looking for a young missing girl. I wondered if it was your friend Margaret he talked about, but I couldn't get much out of him and he never came back after that.

"I looked for you every day for a time. Asked around about you. Where have you been? I haven't seen your Pa neither since then. It was about a month after the constable came looking for you that the new couple moved in. I've been so worried about you, love."

Mrs Evans never knew about Agnes but Hannah could imagine that the constable nabbed Pa when he went for the ransom and then came looking for Agnes. Of course, since Agnes returned home later that day there was no reason for the constable to come back after that.

Poor Pa. He must have been taken to jail and sentenced to prison. Or to a workhouse. He would have been devastated that she never looked for him, never visited him. Did he know that she had taken Agnes home before even finding out whether or not he retrieved the ransom? What a betrayal that was. And now, two years on, here he was standing in front of her.

She pushed the bun into a paper bag, and, summoning all her courage, she raised her head and looked him direct in the eyes.

"That will be one penny, please," she said.

Pa nodded and fumbled in his pocket. "You – look well, Hannah" he said tentatively.

"Thank you." Hannah's voice was cool but calm. "I am very well."

"Good. I – " He cleared his throat. "I'm glad of that."

There was an awkward silence. Hannah put the bag down on the counter top, and took the penny. She held Pa's gaze steadily. Finally he looked away, and shoved the bag into the pocket of his coat.

"Well, I'll see you about then," he mumbled. He grunted, and left the shop.

Hannah leaned against the counter, feeling the blood swirl in her head. But when her heartbeat settled and she got her breath back, she gave a short sudden nervous laugh.

"What's so funny?" Mrs Grainger demanded, poking her head in.

"Nothing, ma'am."

"Then come here and attend to this dough, it ain't going to knead itself."

Hannah went back and began to knead the heavy white dough, and a smile still hovered around her lips.

৩৯৩

ON HER WAY HOME FROM WORK THAT EVENING, HANNAH passed a little girl in a doorway. There was a dog with her, a small scrappy black creature with ragged ears and a tail like a feather duster, and a box that shook and rocked in such a way that Hannah stopped to look at it.

"Puppy, miss?" the little girl said hopefully. "Good strong beasts, every one of 'em, real fierce, real good ratters." She lifted the lid, and inside were five puppies, each one a different pattern of black and white, and ragged as their mother. They nosed Hannah's hand, and one of them began licking her thumb and making small urgent whimpers in its throat.

"They're not fierce," Hannah said. She looked up at the little girl, and grinned. "They're soft as butter. How much for one?"

"Two shillings," the girl said boldly. "Not a penny less."

Hannah looked at her for a moment, then, shaking her

head, she pulled out her purse. "You're too good at this," she told her, and the little girl's face lit up with a smile as she tucked the coins away.

Hannah picked up the puppy that licked her thumb, and held it against her chest. It had a smoother coat than its siblings, and one of its ears was folded against its head while the other stuck straight up like a flag. It had a splash of white on its muzzle, and a white body and paws in contrast to the black fur surrounding its eyes like a bandit.

It stretched up to lick her chin, its little tail thumping frantically against her arm, and Hannah laughed.

"What you going to call her?" the little girl asked. "She's a girl puppy."

"Agnes," Hannah said softly, tickling under the puppy's lopsided ears. It gave a little whine, and she lifted it higher in her arms, cupping its back legs and wrapping it in a corner of her shawl. It settled there quite happily, and Hannah carried on her way home with one hand reaching into the shawl to touch her puppy's back, stroking the soft line of its spine and feeling its warm happy peaceful life brush against her fingers.

THE END

ABOUT THE AUTHOR

Tillie Walker is an emerging author of historical Victorian romance and family sagas.

Tillie grew up in Tring, Hertfordshire, UK and lived in London for a decade before retreating back to the English countryside. She studied history and literature at university and used her knowledge as a volunteer tour guide at some of London's most visited landmarks.

Strolling the famous streets of London led to her interest in writing historical fiction set in the Victorian period.

My favourite author growing up was Charles Dickens which was a primary reason for choosing my majors at university. I hope my stories will give readers a vivid sense of what it was like in the late 19th century in England.